Yellow Ball
Molly Bang

Morrow Junior Books
New York

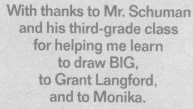

With thanks to Mr. Schuman
and his third-grade class
for helping me learn
to draw BIG,
to Grant Langford,
and to Monika.

Pastels and some tempera were used for the full-color art.
The text type is 42 point Folio Medium.

Copyright © 1991 by Molly Bang

Inquiries should be addressed to William Morrow and Company, Inc.,
105 Madison Avenue, New York, NY 10016.
Printed in Singapore at Tien Wah Press.
1 2 3 4 5 6 7 8 9 10
Library of Congress Cataloging-in-Publication Data
Bang, Molly.
Yellow ball / Molly Bang.
p.   cm.
Summary: During a beach game, a yellow ball is accidentally tossed
out to sea, has adventures, and finds a new home.
ISBN 0-688-06314-4.—ISBN 0-688-06315-2 (lib. bdg.)
[1. Balls (Sporting goods)—Fiction.]   I. Title.
PZ7.B2217Ye 1991   [E]—dc20   90-46077   CIP   AC

To David

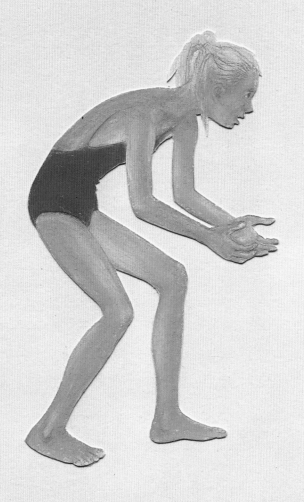

Catch

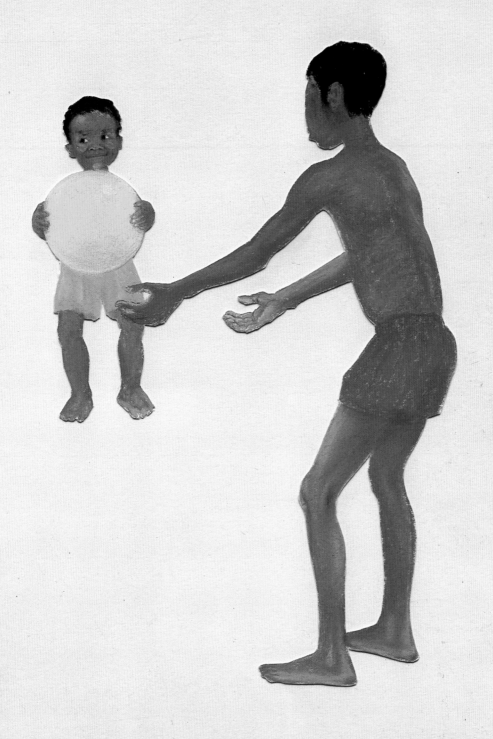

Throw

Uh-oh

Too late now

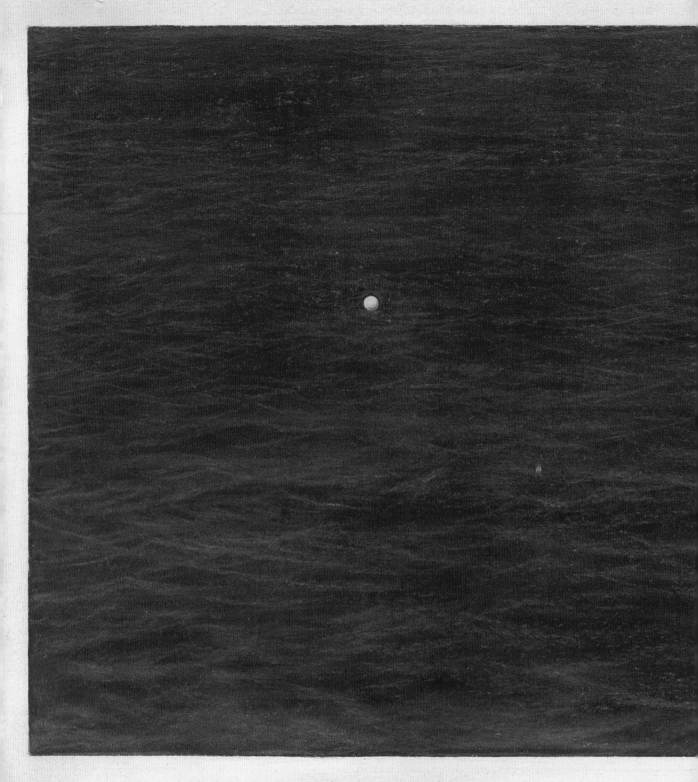

The sea is so big

High   Low

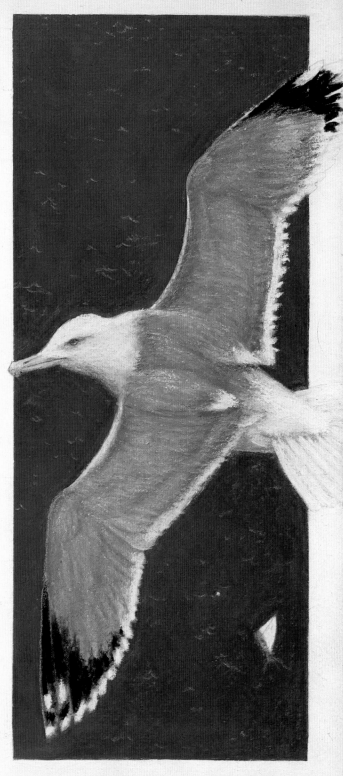

Above

Below

Wind blowing

Storm growing

Watch out!

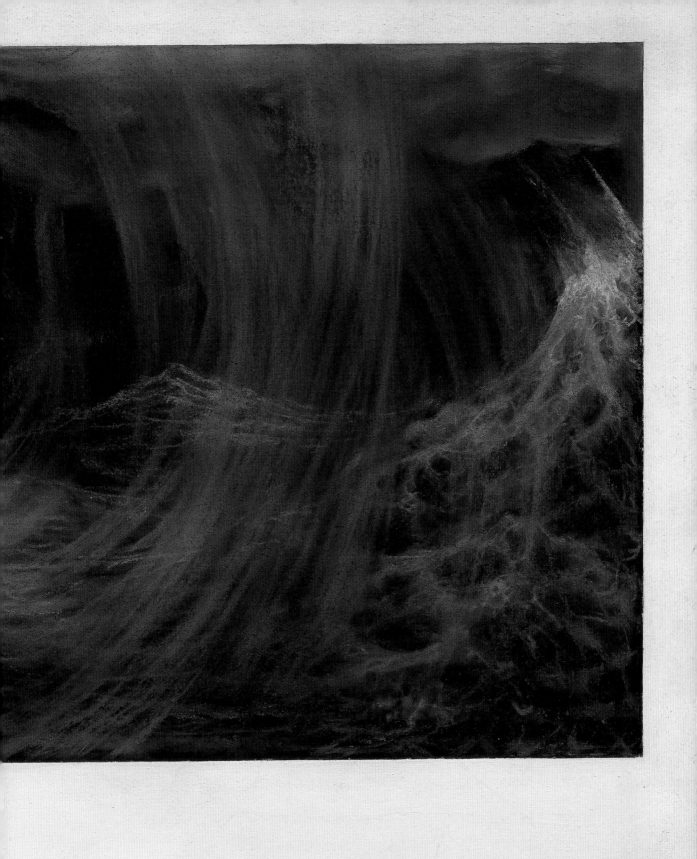

Quiet now

Coming ashore

Look

Hug

Home